Poetry Collection

Shunned

how love of self became my redemption

by Patricia C. Daway

Shunned

how love of self became my redemption

ISBN 978-1-77136-885-8

First Edition: June 2020

Published by
Mélange Magazine Publications
300-3665 Kingsway
Vancouver, BC.,
Canada V5R 5W2
www.readmelange/books.com
Printed in Canada

Cover & Layout Design
Torrez M. Joseph (Ras AQuARii)
Neter Studios
neterstudios@gmail.com
www.torrezjoseph.com

In loving memory of dearest grandmother

Christobelle Brade née Daway

Your endearing love
planted the hope for which I stand

ACKNOWLEDGEMENTS

Locked down and strapped in Toronto, I had no choice but to stay put and reflect. During my reflections, memories of poems I wrote in the early 2000's when jarred by unsettling 3:00 am thoughts, resurfaced. COVID-19 allowed me time for introspection where I allowed specific persons entry into my world.

During this period, those of you who interacted with me, whether for a quick chat, joke, inspiration or spreading love, I say thank you. That interaction with you provided me with encouragement, clarity of thought and gave me the impetus to complete this book.

Much love to my dear friend Alynthia Pierre and family in Toronto, for your kindness and hospitality. My cousin in the British Virgin Islands, Anthony Daway, you have been my constant source of encouragement. We have always looked out for each other, for our life's circumstances were very much similar. I am truly grateful for your support. Alfred Ryan, my dear friend in Toronto who, unwaveringly, stood in as a big brother, and Mitch Rodney in New York, my good friend and sounding board. God knows how much I love you my brothers.

My longtime school friend Danielle Jeffers-Adeyemi, a big thank you for your honesty and critical review.

I must extend a special thank you to my graphic designer, Torrez Joseph, who work with such precision and love.

Last but not least, Debbie Austin with Mélange Magazine Publications, you are a true inspiration. I felt your spirit of trueness from our first encounter back in 2018. When I approached you to publish this book, there was no doubt in my mind of you being the chosen one. You have such discernment that I haven't come across in a while. You understand me, my drive and my direction. Such level of consciousness and harmony working together is a divine gift. Thank you so much for providing a window of opportunity for me.

CONTENTS

PREFACE

It got to a point in my life when I thought I didn't have anything to offer. But the highs and lows of my career path were my only constant buffer. Though I grew up without a mother and a father, I was raised by my virtuous grandmother who departed from my life at a time I wasn't actually prepared for.

Growing up was tough. In the eyes of many, I wasn't expected to be much. I decided to prove them wrong from early as my primary school playground. But as my youthful days and best years quickly got rough, a minute part of me couldn't help questioning whose words I should trust.

Although my circumstances didn't always look favorable, my only hope was knowing that God was always able. During the early stages of adulthood, I realized I had a lot of issues that plagued on the inside since childhood. It took what seems like years of reconstructive surgery to work through them and love of self, to pardon them.

In the midst of my quest for happiness and love, and as broken and dejected as I was, consciously I worked on myself, mentally, emotionally and spiritually. The process took a very long time, but I took that time to understand, know and appreciate loving me. The determining factor was, I could not give up on the goddess in me.

I'm saying this to say that the things we may desire most in our lives often comes with a price. But if we are going to choose to stand for something, be that reflection, there's no need to think twice.

There will even come a time when you may have to walk some journeys alone. But I'm here to tell you don't lose sight of the lane that's your own. We were made to create life, so whatever we do or say, or not do or say, is our contribution – our experiences that may impact someone someday.

Sometimes fear alone or numerous factors tend to hinder our dreams and desires. However, we've got to understand that we are our only true salvation, with the power to choose and be that of God's creation.

So, in spite of my arduous journey, I couldn't dare give up even when I grew weary. It's been my hope to understand the purpose of this journey; for this I disclosed to be my life's story.

Now I can exhale and live as intended, as what I believe to be God's master plan is being creatively orchestrated.

I give utmost praise and gratefulness today to The Most-High Elohim for never giving up on loving me.

The foundation on which I stand:

$$\text{Tribulation } \frac{\text{Determination + Faith}}{\text{HOPE}} = \text{LOVE}$$

PART ONE
SHUNNED

Contribution

What were the chances of my thriving soul
Deemed to be whatever it was born into
The product of my environment decided on its shape
For which I vowed it will not be my truth

I worked hard academically
Fought relentlessly for my steps
Spawned from a drive none can quite understand
With a passion that was consistently frowned upon

Though I was constantly faced with challenges
My soul finally bloomed into its beautiful flower
Though there are still some
Who would go to lengths to see it wither

Vital Source

why was it so distant
why couldn't I reach it
why couldn't I touch it
why couldn't I see it

why wouldn't it hear me crying
why wouldn't it dry my tears
why wouldn't it answer my calls
why wouldn't it share itself

where was it
i looked for it
i begged for it
it promised to come back for me

to protect me
to teach me
to hug me tightly
to kiss me on my forehead

how could something so precious be precarious
how was I to know its absence would be my present
or affect how I navigate my tomorrow
why wasn't I warned, taught, protected

perhaps you didn't know it either
so how could your love share itself to me when you
desperately needed it too
in spite of the absence of love for which I now understand
i had to come to terms with you were merely protecting
me from your own anguish too

i knew more about your sorrow than you as my mother
from a distance you provided, so I knew you cared;
though words I needed to hear, even sparingly,
still thankful you gave me life for which you sacrificed
so I could go beyond and strive.

in thoughtful memory of my mother
Mildred "Lynette" Daway

Not My Life

Out of my wounds bore the hurt of pain
Waves of sorrow, shame and disdain
Caught in humiliation, depression and rejection
The unwavering tears of my inner reflection

It wasn't always this way
It started, then it stopped and again today!
But it was too late you know
I was already deep in the belly of woe

Blinded by blinkered tears of betrayal
Mind the gap _____
Ooh now I'm trapped!
It's such a dark place!

Aaargh!

What was that!
Slippery!
Nothing to hold on to...!
No inspiration!
No motivation!
No peace!
No joy!

Help me!
I need direction!
A touch!
An ear!
What it's worth this time?!

Know the Wiles

I don't care that you don't stay in touch
That doesn't really bother me as much.
The fact that I am here
And you are the reason I am,
Left to wonder how sincere was your plan.

Was this your idea all along?
Or the whispers in your ear was the favorable song?
Enthralled not, by your lies
Much to your dismay, it's what I despise
Or is this the silly games you play for my demise?

Victim Eyes

Lost?
Am I?
Am I?
Am I?

Just a mere morsel
With a bottle or two;
Then came an eviction notice
And the bills too.

With no one to talk to because they say you always **dey pon de past**
So, left with no clarification for there was no one to ask.
Your friends start talking about you.
Surprise, surprise! Your colleagues undermining grew
And there goes the backs of your own family too.

You tell the truth no one believes you;
Perhaps they're scared because they know the truth too.
You offer to help but your kindness gets trodden on,
No matter where you turn it's like you don't belong.
You're described as weird for being misunderstood,
Ultimately shunned by a society that deems to be too good.

Then the only one who unreservedly loves you dies,
Left with no sense of direction but to wonder why.
Your body aches being in constant despair
For being different, as it has now appeared.
There is beauty in variety if they'd took the time to care.
Now it's about protecting self from the pain that lives out there.

My Rear Quest

THE CRY
Living in organized chaos, literally confused.
Under the radar was physical, emotional and other abuse.
Led by misconceptions and deceptions;
Misguided by nurturers and wretched counsellors

Trapped and entombed under a clutter of lies
Not knowing who I was under the disguise
Afraid yet personify bravery, who was I kidding?
Yet unknowingly shielded by God from total ruin.

Buried under layers of hurt, anger and loneliness
Securely fenced in with no near sign of closeness
Barely knowing love or the demonstration thereof
Oh, how my soul cried out to the Creator above.

THE CHILD
The cares of the world became my worry
In spite of the odd childhood fun and games,
The pilferer lurked stealthily for my future, for my days
Left me self-reviled and forced into half-crazed
My mind and body desperately conflicted,
Masked were the sorrows rapt painfully in vulnerability.
A bird's wing was a welcomed and longing opportunity.

YOUNG ADULT
Though living away from home
I assumed responsibilities that were not my own
The relentless desire to be a part of became my dire quest,
Inevitably met with manipulation and so much distress

So tempted to take a rest
From my deepest woes I silently wept.
Trenched in hope to be swept away, I hung in there
for another day.

WOMANHOOD

Yes, I've made it! I'm well-travelled! I've got it together!
I know what I want now so it should be better.
A soft voice firmly exclaimed, *wait, not so quick!*
There were important things I have missed
Apparently, an essential necessity for life capability
Also, the requirement for any peaceful soul sustainability
Love of self! That's what it is! Taken away at the beginning
It defines and unfolds the chart to abundant living
Teach me this one; and so, my new quest begun
Though I never gave up on the former one.

SELF-CARE

Losing the only one I knew who cared
From two generations of old
Have left me bewildered for a while there, out in the cold
With unbearable strain weighing on my parched soul
I desperately reached out in daze before I was a year old
To who showed no interest or proclivity to care,
So I accepted the reality of my heart's affair
And carried on my quest of love and self-care.

LOVE AT LAST

Faced with what seems like unrealistic realities;
The battles of the mind released its unwelcomed qualities.
Indistinct courage persuasively weathered the encounter.
Anchored in hope, in came passion and took over;
Reclaiming the love this journey desperately lacked.
Thank you, My Creator, for always having my back
This ultimate quest has been my life's long request.
No doubt an arduous journey that has put me through the test.

On My Knees

Oh, gates of heaven are you open today?
I fall on bended knees to pray
Even when I know not what to say.

Today, it is myself I cannot forgive
Tribulations too dire
Have distorted my vision on how to live!

Lift my soul from condemnation
Heal my heart from indignation
Thank you, for bearing my supplication.

Yes, my child I am open today, and 24 hours every day
I have heard and answered your prayer all day
Know it is done and so will be, in time to come.

Resilience

I'm here! I'm there!
Am I where I am?
Living? Or am I?
Where? Somewhere!
Why, I don't know?
What? In time!
It's the journey,
I have to go!

I have gotten so used to going,
That it would be a problem staying.
There's nothing you can say about why I'm leaving.
Though sometimes I do try to find a reason,
But nothing was substantiating enough for even a day.
However, if and when I do disobey,
The significance for staying was far too much to pay
So, now I simply go without delay.

You wouldn't understand, Nor should you.
My purpose was always part of a much bigger plan.
I don't expect you to extend a hand;
Or support me even if you can.
Though I'm not delighted by your act,
I knew that's how you'd react.
I'm going now, so never mind that.

Numerous times I have been told,
Remember that you are getting old.
Stay in one place and settle down
And stop the travelling up and down.
Find stability, it needs time;
Give your family, the job, the country and him more time!
But Lord knows how hard I've cried whenever I've tried.
So, I go, because it's just too many times I've been denied.

Each journey's place and space personified as home
Were often filled with just refutations alone,
So I travel to where I can be anonymous as protection
To conceal myself from tireless rejection.
My experiences felt like part of an ultimate master plan
Whenever I take the calls that connect to my spirit man.
Though I may be given years, months, weeks or days
It is still often an uneasy call to take
As I make the preparations that tends to keep me awake.

The journey has taught me to love, including me
But especially those who have taken advantage of me.
To forgive those who have deliberately used me
And ignore those who have truly lied to me.
No more inner struggle of being led by social influence.
After having tapped into my higher spiritual conscience,
I live unapologetically as an introverted empath
With pedantic ways of an intuitive advocate.
In retrospect, all along it was life's creative master plan
To undergo this journey to be groomed as the goddess that
I AM!

Self-Love Actualization I

Most of our lives lived trying to please others

What was the sense if still being criticized

Then came the realization of self-actualization

Either way, let self be of your own perpetuation

PART TWO

REDEMPTIVE LOVE

Self-Redemption

How far will one go;
To embrace it;
To know it;
To see it;
Live it;
Be it;
Don't give up on it?
Recognize the wiles in disguise.
And keep pressing on in loving yourself.

Be True to Self

Could there be anything that we're guilty of;
Caged minds, own victim, all because of?
The glamour and glitter are all great distractions,
The I Am inside cringed at the mass succession.

In spite of the dictation and influence,
Out you tried, but they say you're a nuisance.
Now you're deemed to be under mainstream stress,
To seek psychiatrist and the rest.
What were once your belief, is now under arrest.

Purloined

It was taken away
From zero to seven
No longer of your nurturers
Nor of yourself

Time revealed the manipulation
Sought truth to know thy self
Though 'twas a challenge
Now being rewarded for being resilient

Caged

How not to dress or what line to wear
Funny it depends on the colour of the hair
To deciding on the makeup or botox

Influenced by brands;
The car in the drive;
Oh, did I mention about the house size?

The movies watched
The music listened to
Trying to differentiate the church from the club

The food we eat
To the friends you keep
The family I know, was it all genuine though

Love or hate
Friend or foe
Why the challenge to determine what direction to go?

Seek higher self
Instead of sabotaging yourself
Let your soul visualize and allow true love to be actualized

Relate or Ship

you claimed to love me so much,
why wouldn't your arms hold me at my weakest;
or your eyes see the beauty within at the ugliest;
or why wouldn't your heart move at my worst.

one day I thought you were the best thing that
has happened to me;
another day I thought you were the worst thing that could
have happened to me;
today I think that you were neither the best nor the worst
you just weren't for me; we were never meant to be!

It's Ok

I'm not afraid anymore
I'm with Him now
You may wonder how I know that
But that has been my cry
You just never hear me

Though everyday has been an uphill battle
Deep down I knew why
But I dealt with it in my own way
Nevertheless, I had my hopes and dreams
That one day I wouldn't have to live this way

God sees, knows and operates through our hearts
And how I long for Him to stop mine from tearing apart
Hope my sins are forgiven and you have forgiven me too
For I will not cross this path again
I am not afraid anymore

In memory of my Uncle John
September 21, 2011

Valour

Don't run in someone else's lane

Or compromise your good to get a name.

Why slot into a criterion to fit in as a meme,

Or how far would we go to obtain fame-(us) opportunity?

Don't you see we are losing our integral ability?

Five for the dollar but what's the sense;

Live for self and not as someone else.

There's a plethora of genuineness left for organics,

Don't be quality-struck by the glamour of synthetics.

Honey Be

Aren't you fed up with people trying to curb you into their else;
Who is this someone else?
Could it just be their unseemingly unattainable self?
Appropriate thyself for the love of self

Special are you,
How could you not conceive?
My eyes behold your inner strength
My heart perceives your soul

Your smile exudes fearless courage
The rays of your subtle humility affect nations
You are not just the letters of your songs
You are creation, of relevant substance

The world sees just a fraction of our Trueness
It wants to find us even guarded by genuineness
Strip thoughts of today, yesterday and tomorrow
I dare you to be audacious in your attempt

Be disciplined; yes, self!
Walk circumspectly; yes, so cautious!
Refueled by the Universe; yes, your provision!
You are good! Yes, you are enough!

Self-Love Actualization II

Why not be,
Who else would you rather be?
Who wants to be you;
Who wants to be me?
Wouldn't you want to know you or
What it's like to just be?!

PART THREE
SELF LOVE

Whose Reality

How important is your Life?
Have you chosen to live or be a sacrifice?
Would you consider your steps on this quest influenced?
What does it take to be yourself?

We were told that the most important factor to learn are the
lessons from this life
But how and when do we recognize them without having
to live it twice?
Sadly, it is one of the most challenging issues faced
on life's journey
But if we stop to look around, consequence of these acts can
ne'er be found.

What is the key to life we seek, to be and act in accordance of
Is it not the renowned gift packaged as love as we hoped?
For which most has never had the pleasure to experience nor the
desire thereof
Yet, anxiously it awaits to assume its natural role
But how can we live up to the vast accountability it upholds?

From womb to birth we were mere innocents
So at what stage were we strangers by influence,
And on what account have we decided we were different?
Perhaps we should ask oneself, how did we get into this
predicament?

Why and who has decided to subjugate such precious gift by the
measure of skin tone,
Or has it been concluded that we were not created from the
same bone?

Who has decided on the rays of inequality
Starred in religion, culture, politics or dare I say socially?

Can you see the problems that broods the "Who's & Why's"?
Need we complain about the way the world is today?
Shouldn't we be living as we truly desire?
Or is it because we are too afraid to stand up to the empire?

Living in the shadows of the "Who's & Why's"
Contributors or distributors same difference and cry
We allowed our gift to be damaged and displaced
And our behaviours repellent with much disgrace

Can we find our way back to the noble truth of love
And identify ourselves to what it constitutes of,
Or are we too embedded in the acts of the "Who's & Why's"
That we no longer know the recognition of such love to even try?

Why have we allowed this to go on from generation to generation;
Another innocent nurtured in this way?
Or is it not enough to see how these acts are destroying the world
we live in today?
Perhaps it's true, but what can we do, you say?

I say, embrace sense of self!
And live as truth intended!
Be human!
Personify Love itself!

Enchanted Embrace

Not for anyone

But first for self

Then you'll know how to truly love someone else

Know the existence starts from within

And that's how true refining also begins

It will exude beauty that's worth waiting

Love's Growth

Not too preoccupied to hear the silent cries
Dignified by the world's colorful canvas
Lured by the isms visibly recognized

Relinquish despair, sketch with your own tools
You are equipped, you just didn't know it
Create your art of joy with passion

The eyes of the soul distinguish its colour
Guided by its instinctive power
Conveyed through the heart's welcoming portal

Anchored and Robust!
Infinite yet Precious!
Inevitable still Ubiquitous!

Charter on!
Stay focused!
In love's natural habitat!

Love's Anatomy

It's hard to express the sincerity of one's heart
To anyone who cannot see its feature is state-of-the-art
The anomaly to believe its anatomy can exist platonically
Still gets blinded by its obvious difference
Though packaged in its natural essence
However, unrecognized by conformism,
This precious virtue stays trapped in fundamentalism.

What determines true love,
Whose love is sincere
And, to whom do you share?
You are told to love
But it gets taken advantage of
Worldly influences coerce the majority at best,
But the discerning spirit knows whose to test.

Love in its purest form needs no law.
To gain the purity of such love is a rare pleasure.
Look beyond the rubble, see through its lenses;
No worldly dictations, knowledge or influences.
It was once a given but relinquished by worldly power
But can now only be recognized by those who know its
honour.

Enact this love to permeate naturally
In its rightful order, unconditionally
Serves in its divine purpose for our existence
As it's also a requirement for our soulful sustenance.
Let the purpose be fulfilled and in our pursuit of doing so,
Allow the love of God to truly flow.

I am thankful for true Love's anatomy!
It does not flee from you nor give up on me.
It looks beyond our potential and sets us free.
Up from the rubble to a much higher level,
What a beautiful treasure one ought to keep.
Oh, but not so quick, it's our due diligence to share it
so we could reap.

Love Knows You

It's natural self
Who else?

I can only be love
My soul knows no other

Don't let people put conditions on you
Nor you on another

The answer is true love
Not disparity

Love does not ride with ego
Nor does it pretend with fake

Love authenticity
Patience not reactivity

Bearing the characteristics of true love
You can only be in accordance thereof

Stand for Something

What do you do when your efforts are shunned
For trying to help your fellowman
Suggesting how to be one's best
Not in correlation with the rest

Knowing love extends beyond oneself
Thus, always willing to help someone else
So why the contemplation of self-ruin
When we should be grooming more pillars for our youngins.

Facets of Our Soul (I)

Life permeates through the depth of our soul
in its divine essence
Wisely anchored by our higher conscience
Deeply affected by our thinking
Be mindful of who we let in or what we have plug in

Through the process of achieving any desired results
It begins with conceived thoughts no doubt
Followed by the course of perceived thinking
Supported with sound knowledge not allegedly seeking
Manifested self-awareness but understanding being the purest

Finally, the process of decision-making;
Coupled with the willingness to act on the next step
Standing courageously to appropriate wisdom
If done correctly, radiates from a place of love
With divine faith steering along

Facets of the Soul (II)

Know the I Am of your soul
Understand the morals it upholds
It's time we live not as the me
Or conditioned by this world we see
Rise, let's give our soul the chance to be!

The soul needs no grandeur applause to perform
On the contrary, its natural core is already extraordinary.
Unconditional love is the organic recipe
Enabled with the grandest ability to choose whatever you
wish to be.

An Expression of Resilience

Defeated by the lies
Stifled tears smile back
Bright eyes masked what it knows
Cracked tone knows its own

My heart calls your name
It knows no other
It burns, then swells
Tears don't fall

Tomorrow arrives
So much to be thankful for
Aesthetics of profession, beauty and gain
Academics, entrepreneurship, they're all the same

There are rules
Yet too many games
Know the difference
Keep your heart open

It is there
Whether in black and white
Though a grey area
Whatever you choose, let it matter!

Awaken

What am I for interpretation?
I could see what I'd like to do
But there is this bridge,
Not easily accessible

It is such a vigorous process
To attain this level of consciousness.
Though I can clearly see what I want to do,
It can seem so unattainable

Writing my vision makes me happy
Reassures me it will be there for me when I'm ready
But why am I not yet ready?
What is it are you trying to tell me?

Energy is everything; Everything is energy,
Trapped energy affects the oscillation of such vibration
I watched that which motivates my inspiration
Just up and decided to take a vacation

The Universe appropriate our needs timely
Wake up! Get up! Do things wisely!
Funny enough I was betwixt and between mind
Subjective to my inner perspective
Aware that keeping it in context is so imperative.

Self-Love Actualization III

Whenever I listen to certain genre of music

My soul would come alive, happy and enthusiastic

Go about my day joyfully content

Fully embracing being in my element

PART FOUR
MY SUNSHINE

Shine On

Take time out for Meditation
Nurture your Spirit
Now is a good time to reveal it
Highlights of our flawed world clearly on display
Do not be consumed by what's going on today
Renewed strength comes forth when one is still
Meditation births new energy all at your will

Life's Gift

This Gift!
My Life!
Packaged in Love!
Is the only treasure I can think of
As a precious contribution that should not be used for the
guiles of conformism.
Empowered to allow this beautiful gift to grow,
Until it's my time to naturally go.

A Joyful Soul

Where do I find truth?
About God?
About self?
About everything?
Who can I trust; who might actually know something?

Don't know what to pray much less the power of prayer.
I'm so baffled that I forgot meditation was out there
The willingness surfaces now and again
But soon gets suppressed from lack of creativity within

Oh, how I yearned night and day for peacefulness
and simplicity
Maybe because I lacked spiritual awareness
and acceptance alike
Yes, I would like to know more about affirmation
So I could make better choices for spiritual conservation
But what about true freedom, wouldn't that be fun?

I read if I surrendered to God there would be no boundaries.
He is compassionate to my needs
and not to just some degrees.
Now I'm ready for closure of all my infirmities
And live in nonjudgement and forgiveness,
Lord help me please!

I am eager to understand the fullness of service,
Help me dear God to deliver this notice.
I am ready to extinguish the anger that inflamed my life
without warning
And exhale the confusion I inhaled for conforming.
I am ready to cancel on disappointment before doubt sets
in to make an appointment.
But fear rushed in with talks of being lonely,
Knowing what it's like to be unappreciated, I decided on
taking it slowly.

Wow! I can now live a life of authenticity for that I Am
Radiating patience, a characteristic learnt from
the True One.
Stepping out boldly in faith along with courage
and discipline,
Finally, living in my balance, it is never too late
It's an icing I'm happy to regurgitate

Each day I learn expansion beyond myself
Filled with gratitude I choose the order of aptitude
I pray this joy may forever resonate with me
Whilst knowledge, wisdom, understanding beams brightly
Today, I bask in your unconditional love ever so radiantly!

Rededication

From a child I felt suppressed
Because I couldn't be as my soul request
So much to give
Unable to express

Lost in consciousness
For fear of being judged
I learnt it was the way to infiltrate the acts of wrong
Stifled in tears, yearning for the day to be naturally strong

My sacred getaway was always dream time,
When washing the dishes, I leisurely go into overtime.
Imagining living as my soul solicited;
Freedom to be as longingly intended.

My transformation varied from face to place
Some would have it that I was running away
Almost believed that too from one workplace and space
But quickly got dismissed dare I miss my trace

Being deprived for years was perhaps orchestrated
Be where I wanted but never attached
Be what I wanted but not quite intended
Be whom I wanted but never quite that

I can see I was being groomed to be my soul's best
Finally, loving, living my soul's request
This be my rededication, my contribution,
No matter who decline
Truly living the life given as mine, THIS TIME!

Happy Existence

Living a life knowing who I am was quite an awakening,

Built on a relationship with The Divine One.

My existence spurned fruitfully,

Love being my nourishment daily.

Renewed mind!

Restored heart!

I've been protected from the start,

Guarded in His Fortress.

In His Word I take my rest;

My new life rededicated to the world,

Thank you, dear God for redeeming my soul!

Giving Back

Self-love has brought me to this place of enlightenment;
Even though arduous, it was worth it,
As I am a better person for it.

We can become lifetime prisoners of our own mind
should we let it,
To the world we are nothing special unless we sacrifice
our soul,
Inevitably, we judge ourselves so harshly
But we ought to learn of our being and specialty.

I am aware that I Am an expression of the Universe
Operating through thoughts and emotions
Exemplified by temporary human experiences
Not caged by worldly thoughts and actions.

I am that I am.
Energy that transfers
To create an experience for my interpretation
For that of a spiritual purpose and being

Best expressed on the planes of Higher Consciousness
Elevated Vibrations portal Love, Joy and Peace
The element of Enlightenment attained
An originality we all should retain

Year 2020, the era of Awakening
Whether you seek it or not
For it you will be faced
So is your choice to live on one plane

You get in life a reflection of who you are.
It is productive to help people explore who they are
Teach a man how to fish
To maintain sustainable growth for a life time dish

I Am Love

See in love
Speak in love
Share in and with love

Announce love
Answer to love
Allowing love to be

Receive love
Accept Love
Give in and with love

Call on love
Accommodate love
Trust in and with love

Let in love
Freely love
Unite in and with love

Love cannot be created
Nor can it be animated
The manifestation of love is to be love

Wonders of Life

Many of us wonder about life
Most of us wonder about the path we trod
Some of us wonder about our destiny
And all of us wonder about the uncertainties
that befriend us

Questions of "when", "how", "what", "where" and "whom"
encloses our destiny

The "maybes", "could haves if", "would haves but",
clouds our direction

And the "which" and "whys" that leaves our soul panting
for glorification

Hence, who is to say that life's journey isn't a mere fraction
of questions

Questions of life we face as the day unfolds
And the answers we live as the night subdue
So who is to say what it reveals for me or disclose for you
But with convictions so powerful, left disguise are the
wonders within

My Hero

Truly divine
You loved so deep
A love so rare
My heart still skips a beat

But for those who have experienced it
Or knows it well
Will choose to live as such
Without having to be compelled

When I think of you
Or utter your name
Tears still come to my eyes
Even so much as to hear it being claimed

You listen, observe and speak when spoken to
Though soft spoken and quiet, your words still ring true
All I have to do is remember a thing you might do
And that would be my answer too

JAN 11, 1931 - FEB 12, 2006

Your eyes told stories of a virtuous woman who've had
an onerous journey
You show kindness to anyone and cared especially
for your own family
Though imperfectly immaculate
Your humbled spirit remains one I choose to emulate.

Thank you for sharing your life with me
Your love and sacrifice were always my comforting choice
Your perseverance gives me the hope for which I stand
Thank you for being my grandmother, there's so much I
now understand.

Self-Love Actualization IV

I can't allow past pain and jarred experiences,
To be a prediction of life reoccurrences.
True love has no expiry or laws;
Delightfully thrilled to love me and all my flaws

Autobiography

Patricia C. Daway

I was born on the Emerald Isle of Montserrat in 1976 to a Montserratian mother and an Antiguan father, however, raised by a virtuous grandmother.

Although I left home in 1993 at the age of 16 to pursue my studies and furthered ambitions, and left behind a past that availed itself to taunt my days.

Two years after I left home, the volcano erupted in 1995 and obliterated two thirds of the island making it a risky habitat, so I decided not to return home and choose another country to live. Nonetheless, I was always intrigued by the world's diverse cultures. I therefore traveled extensively, living in many countries and cities for nearly three decades, hoping that special one would beguile me into calling it home. Inevitably, my traveling lifestyle branded me "a rollin' stone." It was never meant to be that way, but neither were the experiences of my ramblings.

We all know that life comes with its challenges and we are often thrown into situations where our physical, emotional and mental capabilities are tested. Having encountered a number of barriers that threatened to impede my progress, I managed to stay positive as I journeyed to overcome my challenges. I fought to embrace the hardships whilst I remained steadfast in my steps of persistence and growth, drawn from the strength within.

However, I'm ever so grateful for my writing which has helped immensely along the way. Writing acts as my guide and teacher, allowing me to stop and take stock of where I am, thus enabling me to see the error of my ways. Most importantly, it has empowered me to be a better person on either side of the coin.

As I enthusiastically embrace my re-defined path and contribution; being in a place of redemption makes the impossible appear achievable, and second chances acceptable.

I find this place of presence experientially very therapeutic.

THE ROSE
AND
HER FRIENDS

Juan Jose Gonzalez Jr

ENDING QUOTE

Remember, you are beautiful no matter where you are or who you are with. You are always special.

ACKNOWLEDGMENT

To my mother, Elena Amaya, who gave me permission when I was 13 years old to get up at 2 or 3 in the morning and write down my words.

ABOUT THE AUTHOR

Juan J. Gonzalez is a percussionist, lyricist, and singer, who is also a published poet since 1978.

He's a father, brother, and a grandfather.

His goal is to put in words feelings and expressions for the world that cannot.

His new book "Poems of life" will

be coming out in 2026.

He added,

Then all of a sudden the smooth shiny Stone began to speak,

He also said,

Then the seashell said to the Rose,

She added,

Then the Rose said to the seashell,

And the rose responded,

Then the seashell asked The Rose,

The sea shell responded,

Then she added,

Then the Rose said to the
seashell,

At the same time, a beautiful seashell was swept onto the shore near the same shiny stone.

One day, a Castilian Rose was blown away from its bush and landed on a shiny, smooth stone near the seashore.

DEDICATION

Dedication goes to my nephew and nieces. My beautiful daughter, Sabrina Elisa Gonzalez, and her twins; my grandchildren, Reign Thea and Silas Flynn.